The
DOG THAT DUG

To Ian Hamilton Gordon, K.P.
To Mum, and in memory of Tess the dog, J.L.

A Red Fox Book

Published by Random House Children's Books
20 Vauxhall Bridge Road, London SW1V 2SA

A division of Random House UK Ltd
London Melbourne Sydney Auckland
Johannesburg and agencies throughout the world

First published in 1992 by The Bodley Head Children's Books

Red Fox edition 1993

10

Text © Jonathan Long 1992
Illustrations © Korky Paul 1992

Printed in Hong Kong

RANDOM HOUSE UK Limited Reg. No. 954009

ISBN 0 09 998610 8

The DOG THAT DUG

Jonathan Long and Korky Paul

Red Fox

There once was a dog who was a bit of a clot.
He'd buried his bone and forgotten the spot.

He sniffed round the garden in search of his nibble,
Till he sniffed something nice and started to dribble.

'That must be my bone,' he said, 'down in the muck.
I knew I would find it with a bit of good luck.'

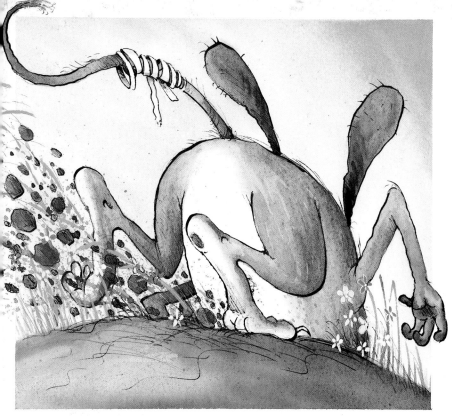

So he stuck in his paws and he scratched and he dug,
Till he found something hard and he gave it a tug.

But when he opened his eyes, guess what he'd found
– it wasn't the bone that he'd left underground –

It was an old brown shoe with a hole in the toe
That someone had dropped a long time ago.

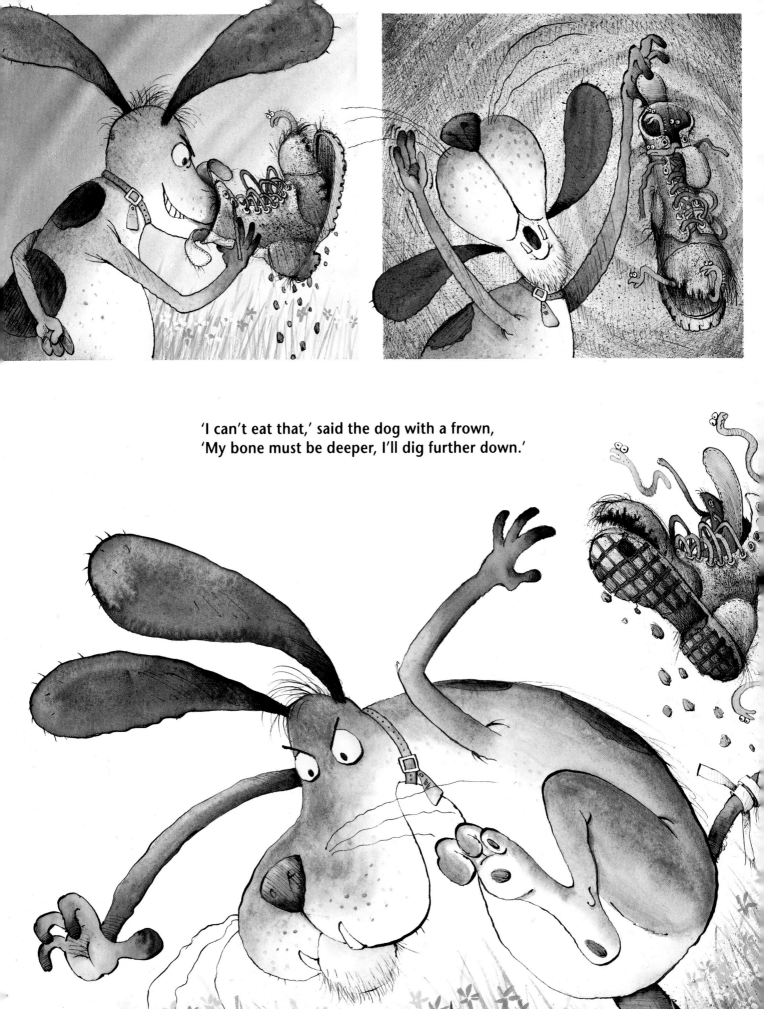

'I can't eat that,' said the dog with a frown,
'My bone must be deeper, I'll dig further down.'

So he stuck in his paws, and he scratched and he dug,
Till he found something else and he gave it a tug.

But when he opened his eyes, guess what he'd found
– it wasn't the bone that he'd left underground –

But a coal-mining miner, all covered in soot,
Very surprised to be tugged by the foot.

'Sorry,' said the dog, 'I do beg your pardon,
I didn't expect to find you in the garden!'

The miner yelled 'Bad boy' and made quite a fuss
Then strode down the road to look for a bus.

'Well I can't eat him,' said the dog with a frown,
'My bone must be deeper, I'll dig further down.'

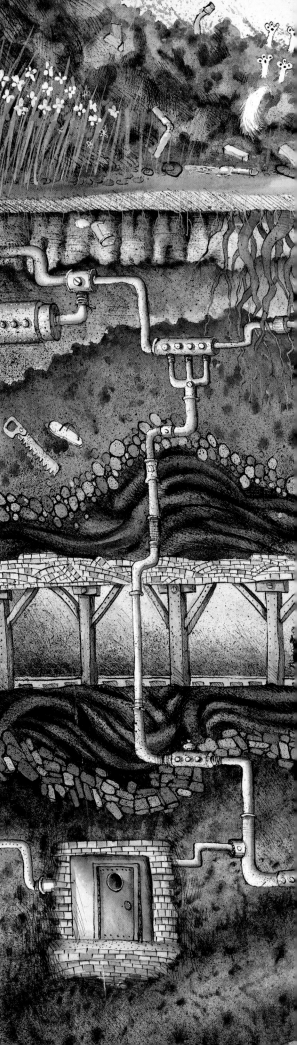

So he stuck in his paws, and he scratched and he dug,
Till he found something else and he gave it a tug.

It was terribly heavy and the dog had to battle,
But at last it came out with a shake and a rattle.

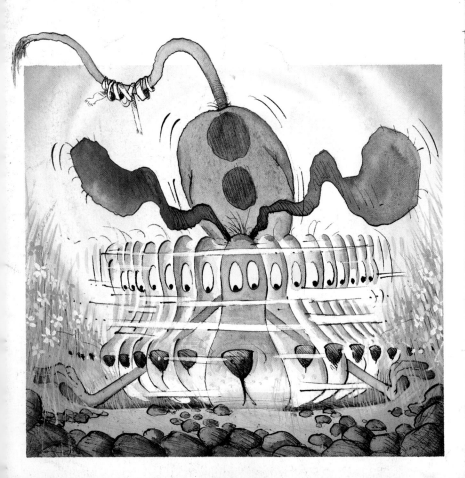

Can you guess what it was, the thing that he found?
A tubular train that chuffed underground!

With twenty-four carriages all full of faces
And a little fat driver in a hat and some braces.

'What are you doing? This isn't my station!'
Shouted the driver with great indignation.

'Sorry,' said the dog, 'I do beg your pardon,
I didn't expect to find you in the garden!'

'Well I can't eat him,' said the dog with a frown,
'My bone must be deeper, I'll dig further down.'

So he stuck in his paws and he scratched and he dug,
Till he found something else and he gave it a tug.

But tugging it out was a terrible strain –
More of a strain than the tubular train.

And when it was out, guess what he'd found,
Buried away deep under the ground –

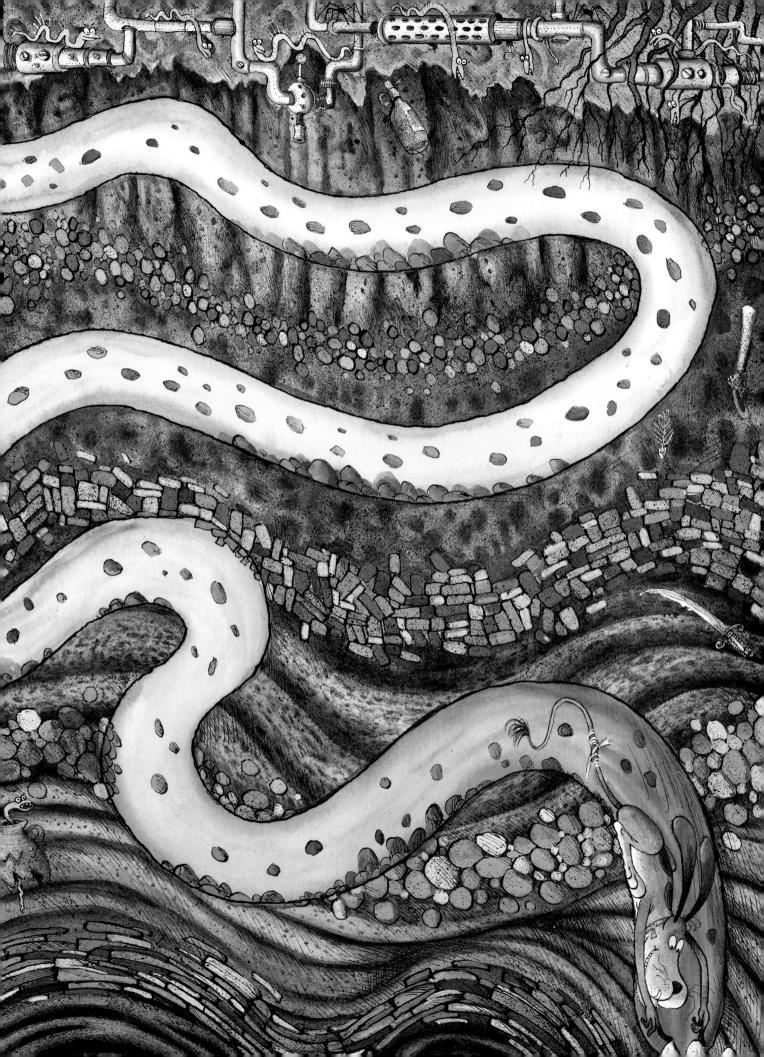

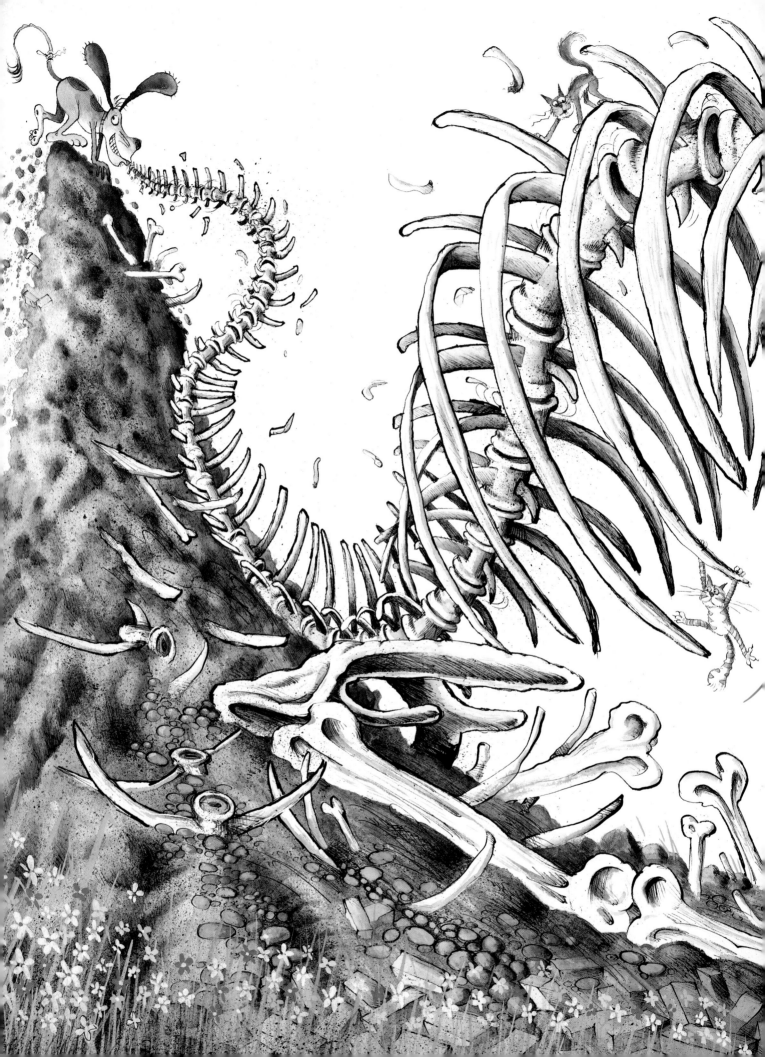

It was a bone at last, but it wasn't a single.
It was joined to some others and they all made a jingle.

There were big bones a-plenty and small ones galore
– all that was left of an old dinosaur.

'What a surprise,' said the dog with a smile,
'This pile of snacks will last quite a while.'

'Wait just one minute,' came a voice from aloft,
'Those bones are rare and not to be scoffed.'

A smiling professor was over his shoulder
With little round glasses and a shabby red folder.

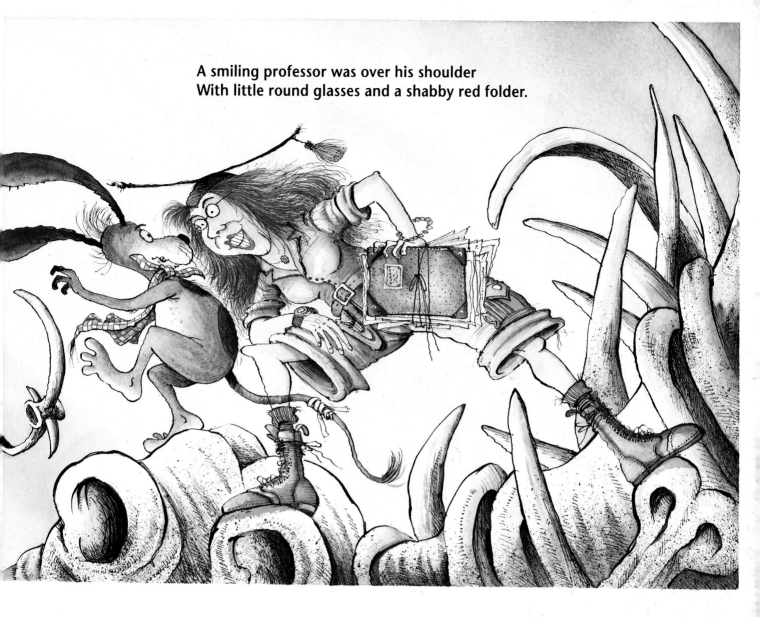

'I'm hungry,' said the dog, 'those bones are my dinner.
If I don't eat them soon, I'll end up much thinner.'

'Look here,' said the prof, 'I'm not being funny,
Give me those bones and I'll give you some money.'

'Great!' said the dog, holding out one of his paws,
'Two million pounds and the bones will be yours!'

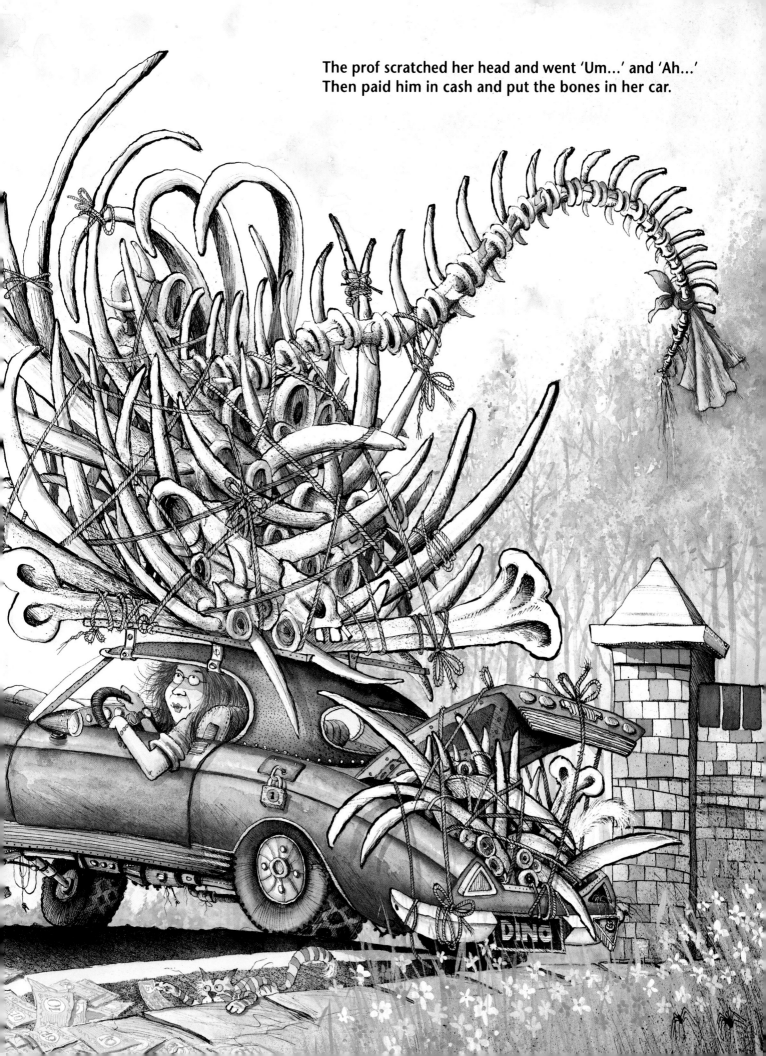

The prof scratched her head and went 'Um...' and 'Ah...'
Then paid him in cash and put the bones in her car.

When she had gone, the dog went to the shops
And bought a pound of his favourite chops.

And steaks and burgers and sausages in strings
And hot spicy pies, and other nice things.

Then he invited his friends for a beautiful dinner,
Where no one had bones – and no one got thinner.

Some
bestselling Red Fox
picture books

THE BIG ALFIE AND ANNIE ROSE STORYBOOK
by Shirley Hughes
OLD BEAR
by Jane Hissey
OI! GET OFF OUR TRAIN
by John Burningham
DON'T DO THAT!
by Tony Ross
NOT NOW, BERNARD
by David McKee
ALL JOIN IN
by Quentin Blake
THE WHALES' SONG
by Gary Blythe and Dyan Sheldon
JESUS' CHRISTMAS PARTY
by Nicholas Allan
THE PATCHWORK CAT
by Nicola Bayley and William Mayne
WILLY AND HUGH
by Anthony Browne
THE WINTER HEDGEHOG
by Ann and Reg Cartwright
A DARK, DARK TALE
by Ruth Brown
HARRY, THE DIRTY DOG
by Gene Zion and Margaret Bloy Graham
DR XARGLE'S BOOK OF EARTHLETS
by Jeanne Willis and Tony Ross
WHERE'S THE BABY?
by Pat Hutchins